# GRANDAD'S ISLAND

for Grandad.

SIMON AND SCHUSTER

First published in Great Britain in 2015 by Simon and Schuster UK Ltd

1st Floor, 222 Gray's Inn Road, London WC1X 8HB

A CBS Company • Text and illustrations copyright © 2015 Benji Davies

The right of Benji Davies to be identified as the author and illustrator of this work has

been asserted by him in accordance with the Copyright, Designs and Patents Act, 1988

A CIP catalogue record for this book is available from the British Library upon request

ISBN: 978-1-4711-1994-1 (HB) • ISBN: 978-1-4711-1995-8 (PB) • ISBN: 978-1-4711-1996-5 (eBook)

Printed in China

10

# GRANDAD'S ISLAND

## Benji Davies

**SIMON AND SCHUSTER**

London   New York   Sydney   Toronto   New Delhi

At the bottom of Syd's garden, through the gate and past the tree, was Grandad's house.

There was a key under a flowerpot and Syd
could let himself in any time that he liked.

One day Syd called round
to see Grandad.

But he wasn't in any
of the usual places.

Then, just as he was about to leave, Syd heard Grandad calling.

"Ah, there you are!" said Grandad. "There's something I want you to see."

Syd carefully climbed up the ladder.
He had never been in Grandad's
attic before.

It was full of old boxes and things that
Grandad had collected from around the world.

At the far end of the attic, Grandad pulled a sheet down from the wall to reveal a big metal door.

"After you, Syd," he said.

Syd turned the handle – CLUNK – and gave the heavy door a push.

Syd found himself standing on the deck of a very tall ship. There was an ocean of rooftops all around.

Grandad pulled a handle.

**BOOOOOOOP!** went the horn
and the ship lurched forward.

"Steady as she goes!" Grandad boomed.

Grandad was very good at steering the ship and kept them on a smooth course across the rolling waves.

Mile after mile all they saw was sea and sky, sky and sea – until, at last, something appeared on the horizon.

"LAND AHOY!" shouted Syd.

They dropped the ship's anchor and
made their way to the shore.
"Grandad, don't you want your stick?" Syd asked.
"No, I think I'll be all right," said Grandad.

In the thick jungle of the island,
it was very hot.
"We must find a good spot for
a shelter," said Grandad.

At the top of the island, where a cool breeze blew through the trees, they found an old shack.

There was a lot to do, but with a little help, they soon had everything shipshape.

They explored the island high and low. At every turn they saw new wonders.

It was the most perfect place.
Syd wished they could stay forever.

But he knew that it would soon be time for them to leave.

"Syd, there's something I've been meaning to tell you,"
said Grandad. "You see . . .

. . . I'm thinking of staying."

"Oh," said Syd. "But won't you be lonely?"

"No... no, I don't think I will,"
said Grandad smiling.

Before he set sail, Syd hugged Grandad one last time. He would miss him very much.

Everyone came to wave goodbye.

Across the waves, the ship chugged and churned.

The journey seemed much longer without Grandad.
But Syd steered the ship safely home.

The next morning, Syd went back round
to Grandad's house.

It was just the same as it had always been.
Except Grandad wasn't there any more.

In the attic it was very quiet.
The big metal door wasn't there –
it was as if it had never been there at all.

Then Syd heard something tapping at
the window. He wondered what it might be.

There on the window ledge,
was an envelope.

Syd carefully prised it open.

for Syd.